TABLE OF CONTENTS

First published by Parragon in 2009
Parragon
Queen Street House
4 Queen Street
Bath BA1 1HE, UK.

ISBN 978-1-4075-6033-5
Printed in China

THE WORLD OF

Cars

Disney · PIXAR

THE STORY OF THE FILM

The biggest car race of the year – the Dinoco 400 – was about to begin. Cars of all makes and models packed the stadium, ready to cheer on their favourite racers.

Rookie Lightning McQueen was in his trailer revving up.

"I am speed," the race car repeated to himself. "I am Lightning."

Finally, he burst into the stadium. Camera flashes went off all around. The crowd went wild!

Meanwhile, The King, who had been the number one champion race car for years, was at the Dinoco stage, surrounded by reporters. His sponsor, Dinoco, had made him famous, but it was time to move on. He was ready to retire and this would be his last race.

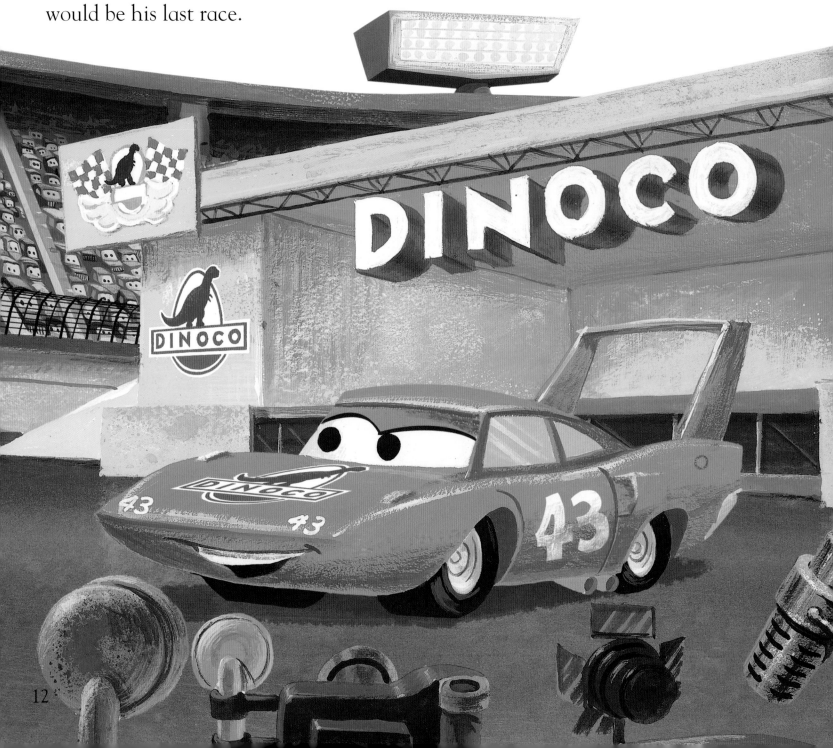

15

Lightning finally drove in for a pit stop.
"No tyres! Just the gas!" he shouted to his crew.
It was a risky move. Too risky.
During the last lap,
Lightning's two
rear tyres blew out!
The King and Chick
quickly closed in on
him. Lightning even
stuck out his tongue to
gain an edge.

"It's too close to call!"
cried the announcer.

While the instant replay was analysed, Lightning boasted to the reporters, "I'm a one-man show."

Furious, his pit crew quit right then and there.

"You ain't gonna win unless you got good folks behind you," The King said to the rookie. "Let them do their job." But Lightning wasn't listening. He was busy dreaming of victory . . .

. . . until the announcer reported that it was a three-way tie! Lightning groaned. He, The King, and Chick would all go to California for a tie-breaker race.

Lightning couldn't wait to win the race and earn the snazzy Dinoco sponsorship.

But for now, he had another sponsor. He rolled into the Rust-eze tent and flashed a forced smile: "Use Rust-eze and you too can look like me!"

Many long hours later, Lightning's driver, Mack, was driving the rookie along the highway to California. Mack wanted to stop for some sleep, but Lightning refused.

"We're driving all night," Lightning insisted.

So the big truck pushed forward. As he fought to keep his eyes open, a gang of cars lulled him to sleep and then began bumping into him. Suddenly, one of the pranksters sneezed. Startled awake, Mack swerved dangerously . . .

. . . and Lightning, asleep in the back, rolled out onto the Interstate! The race car awoke to the sight of traffic speeding towards him. Terrified, he looked for Mack. He thought he saw him going down an exit ramp and quickly followed. But it wasn't Mack!

Lost, Lightning ended up on the old Highway 66.

That was when he noticed flashing lights behind him.

BANG! BANG! BANG! The Sheriff's tailpipe backfired.

"Why is he shooting at me?" Lightning panicked and zoomed recklessly down the main street of a little town, dragging a statue of the town's founder behind him, destroying the road. He stopped only when he got caught between two telegraph poles.

"Boy, you're in a heap of trouble," said the Sheriff.

The next morning, Lightning woke up locked inside the town's impound lot.

"My name's Mater," a friendly tow truck said.

"Where am I?" Lightning grimaced at the rusty truck.

"Radiator Springs," Mater replied proudly. Just then, the Sheriff arrived. It was time for Lightning to go to court.

The courthouse was filled with angry townsfolk. They were upset that Lightning had ruined the road. When the judge, Doc Hudson, saw that Lightning was a race car, he quickly ordered him to leave . . . but then Sally, the town attorney, arrived.

"Make this guy fix the road," the blue sports car said. Sally told everyone that their little forgotten town needed business. Without a road, there would be no travellers, which meant no business.

Doc made his ruling: Lightning couldn't leave Radiator Springs until he fixed the road.

Lightning soon met Bessie – the massive road-paving machine he would have to haul to smooth out the road.

It was no wonder that when Mater took off Lightning's wheel clamp, the race car drove away as fast as he could . . . until he ran out of fuel. The Sheriff had taken the petrol out of Lightning while he was asleep.

With no way to escape, Lightning began to work.

When a minivan couple drove into town, the cars of Radiator Springs shifted into top gear.

"Customers!" shouted Sally.

The cars desperately tried to sell the visitors fuel, tyres, new paint jobs – but the couple just wanted directions to the Interstate.

Later that day, Lightning heard a radio report that Chick was already in California, practising for the race. So the race car pulled Bessie extra hard for one hour, then announced that he was done. But the road wasn't done. It was a mess.

"It looks awful!" exclaimed Sally.

"Now it looks like the rest of the town," Lightning replied rudely.

Insulted, Doc stared long and hard at Lightning. Then he challenged the young hotshot to a race. "If you win, you go and I fix the road. If I win, you do the road my way," he said.

Out at the dirt track, Lightning took a quick lead. But when he made a sharp turn, he skidded into a ditch.

"You drive like you fix roads," said Doc, looking down at the rookie. "Lousy."

34

Humiliated, Lightning went back to work. He scraped up the mess he'd made and started to pave the road once again.

The next morning, the townsfolk awoke to a smooth, newly-paved section of road. Even Doc was impressed. But where was Lightning McQueen?

He was out practising the turn he'd missed when he had raced Doc. Watching Lightning miss the turn again, Doc offered some advice: "Turn right to go left."

Reluctantly, Lightning tried it – and wiped out! Giving up, he returned to paving the road. And as he did, the townsfolk began to spruce up their shops. They were taking new pride in their town.

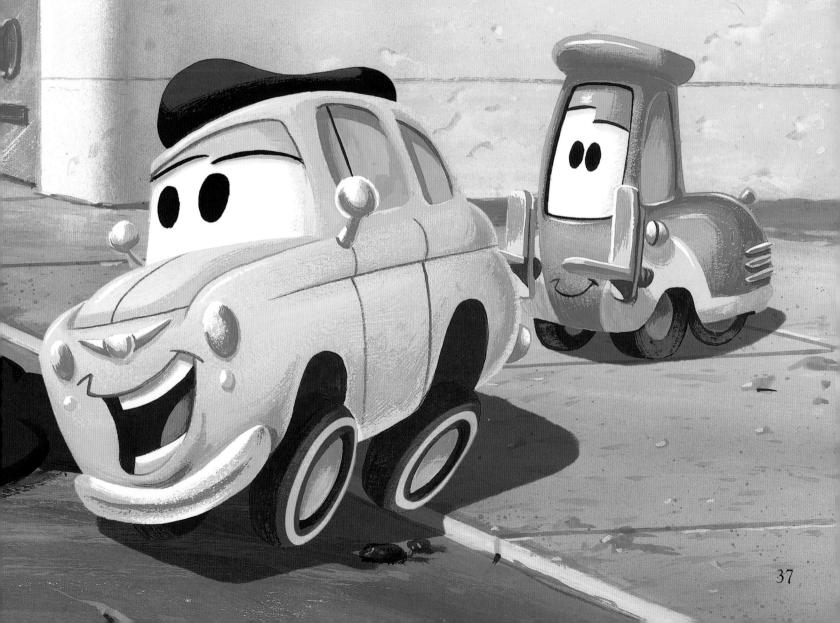

Suddenly, Red the fire engine, sprayed icy cold water on the filthy, cactus-prickled Lightning.

"If you want to stay at the Cozy Cone, you gotta be clean," Sally said. She owned the motel and thought that Lightning might want to stay there instead of at the impound. She was starting to like him and the effect he was having on the town.

"You're being nice to me!" a surprised Lightning said.

That night, Mater took Lightning tractor tipping for fun. Then the truck showed off his backwards driving.

"Maybe I'll use it in my big race," Lightning said about Mater's driving technique. "I'll be the first rookie in history ever to win it. We're talking a big new sponsor with private helicopters. . . ."

Lightning even promised Mater a helicopter ride.

"I knowed I made a good choice," Mater told Lightning.

"In what?" asked Lightning.

"My best friend," said Mater. Lightning smiled as Mater drove away. A best friend!

When Lightning finally drove to Sally's motel, he discovered that she had overheard the conversation.

"Did you mean it? That you'll get him a ride?" she asked, confronting him.

"Oh, who knows?" Lightning said casually.

"Mater trusts you." Sally turned to leave.

"Thanks for letting me stay here!" Lightning said quickly.

"Good night," Sally replied.

The next morning, while Lightning was waiting for his petrol ration, he wandered into Doc's garage. And then he saw a grimy old Piston Cup. The plaque read, The Hudson Hornet, Champion: 1951. There were Piston Cups from 1952 and 1953, too. Lightning couldn't believe it. Doc was a famous race car champion!

When Doc found Lightning, he was furious. "The sign says, stay out!"

"You're the Hudson Hornet! You still hold the record for most wins in a single season!" Lightning babbled.

"All I see is a bunch of empty cups," Doc grumbled as he pushed Lightning outside and slammed the garage door.

Bursting with excitement, Lightning told everyone in town who Doc was. But they all thought he was crazy.

That was when Sally arrived and gave Lightning a full tank of gas. Lightning could have sped out of town . . . but he didn't. Instead, he happily followed Sally through the mountains, finally enjoying the beauty of his surroundings.

"The Wheel Well Motel," Sally said, showing Lightning a broken-down building. "It used to be the most popular stop on the Mother Road."

Then Sally told Lightning that she had been a big-shot attorney in Los Angeles. On a drive across the country, she'd landed in Radiator Springs. It was the first time she had truly felt like she was home.

Sally explained that the big Interstate outside of town hadn't always existed. Before, Highway 66 had been the main road, and in its heyday, it had been something special.

"Back then cars didn't drive on it to make great time. They drove on it to have a great time. Then the town got bypassed just to save ten minutes of driving." Sally sighed. "One of these days we'll find a way to get back on the map."

Later that afternoon, Lightning spotted Doc wearing racing tyres at the dirt track. Ducking out of sight, the rookie watched Doc maneuver effortlessly around the tricky curve that had given Lightning so much trouble.

"Wow! You're amazing!" exclaimed Lightning. Doc turned and raced off.

50

Lightning followed Doc back to his office. "How could a car like you quit at the top of your game?" he asked.

"You think I quit? They quit on me," Doc replied bitterly. Lightning listened as Doc told him about his big wreck. When Doc had recovered, the racing world had told him that he had been replaced by a rookie – a rookie like Lightning McQueen.

The Daily Exhaust FINAL

CRASH!
HUDSON HORNET
OUT FOR SEASON

Season Ender Fender Bender
Puts Young Hornet In Garage

The next morning, a beautiful, newly-paved main road stretched from one end of Radiator Springs to the other.

"Good riddance," muttered Doc, happy that the race car appeared to have finished the job and left town.

But Lightning hadn't left. He became the best customer Radiator Springs had seen in a long time.

He got new tyres, some of Fillmore's organic fuel, supplies at Sarge's, bumper stickers at Lizzie's and a paint job at Ramone's.

"What do you think?" Lightning asked, surprising Sally with his makeover. "Radiator Springs looks pretty good on me."

"It looks like you've helped everybody in town," Sally said gratefully.

On Lightning's cue, the shopkeepers turned on their newly fixed neon signs – just as they had done in Radiator Springs' heyday. It was time to cruise! Everyone slowly and happily drove up and down the street.

It all seemed close to perfect . . .

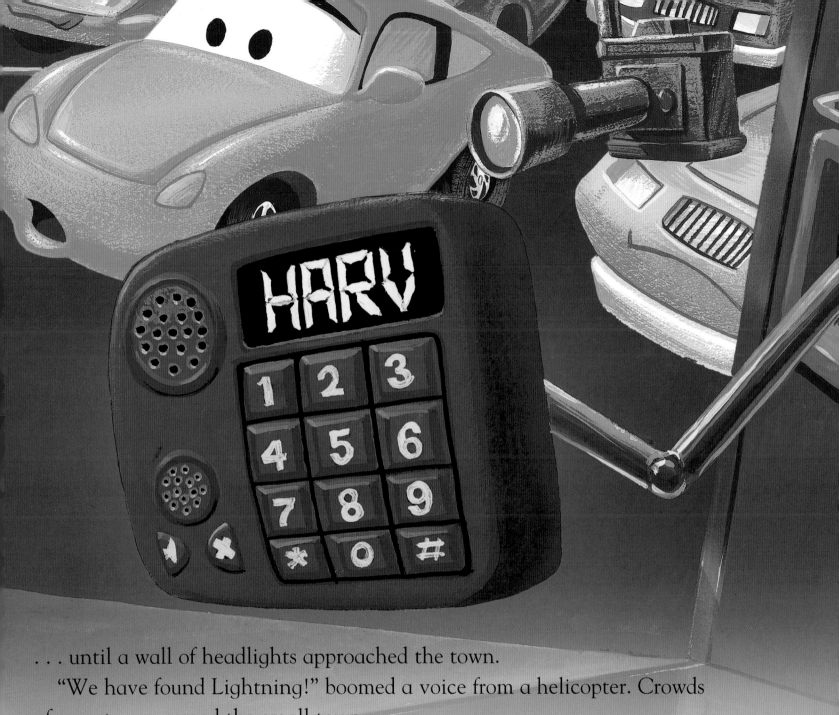

. . . until a wall of headlights approached the town.

"We have found Lightning!" boomed a voice from a helicopter. Crowds of reporters swarmed the small town.

"I'm sorry I lost you, boss," a relieved Mack said as soon as he reached the rookie. And on Mack's speakerphone, Lightning's agent, Harv, told him to get to the race fast:

"Get out of Radiator Stinks now, or Dinoco's history!"

Fighting his way through the reporters, Lightning found Sally. But he
didn't know what to say.
"I hope you find what you're looking for," Sally told him. She turned
and disappeared into the crowd.
"Sally!" Lightning called after her, but it was too late. Sally was
gone, and the reporters were closing in on him.

60

As Mack pulled out of town with Lightning, the reporters followed – except one, who stopped to thank Doc for calling her. Sally was stunned.

"You did this?" she asked.

"It's best for everyone," replied Doc.

"Best for everyone? Or best for you?" challenged Sally.

Radiator Springs was quiet once more.

"I didn't get to say goodbye to him," Mater said sadly.

Everyone but Doc went home silently and turned off the lights. The hope and happiness that had filled the air that night were gone. Doc felt ashamed as he realized how much Lightning had done for their town.

Soon Lightning was at the Los Angeles International Speedway, in the middle of the biggest race of his life. But his heart wasn't in it. The King and Chick were taking over the track. Lightning couldn't stop thinking about Sally and the friends he had left behind.
Suddenly, he found himself headed straight for a wall!

As he recovered, Lightning heard a familiar voice over his radio. It was Doc! All of Lightning McQueen's Radiator Springs friends had come to be his crew!

And when the fans saw that Doc – the Fabulous Hudson Hornet – was the crew chief, they gave a roaring cheer.

Doc focused on Lightning. "If you can drive as good as you can fix a road, then you can win this race with your eyes shut!"

51 FABULOUS HUDSON HORNET

65

Lightning took off with new determination. When Chick bumped him off the track, he used the "turn right to go left" trick. He even drove backwards like Mater.

But just as he was about to cross the finish line and win, he stopped. Chick had caused The King to crash. As Chick zoomed ahead, Lightning sped back towards The King and pushed him across the finish line.

Chick finally won his Piston Cup, but the fans booed him!

Lightning joined his friends at the Rust-eze tent. He had never felt happier. And when Tex, the owner of Dinoco, asked,

"How'd you like to become the new face of Dinoco?"

Lightning graciously said no. He decided to stay loyal to the Rust-eze gang, who had believed in him from the beginning . . . though he did ask Tex for one small favour.

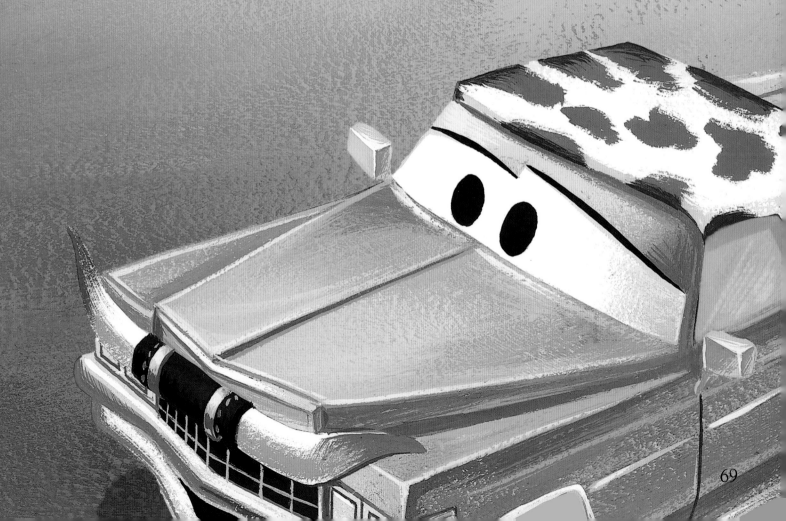

Back at the Wheel Well, Sally was looking out over the valley when she heard a voice say, "I hear this place is back on the map." It was Lightning!

"There's a rumour floating around that some hotshot Piston Cup race car is setting up his big racing headquarters here."

The two cars smiled happily at each other.

That was when Mater came flying by – in a Dinoco helicopter!

"He's my best friend," Lightning said, laughing. Sally smiled. The cocky race car had finally learned about friendship . . . and he'd learned that life was not just about being fast, but also about slowing down to enjoy things.

Lightning McQueen was home at last.

RED'S TUNE-UP BLUES

One morning, Red the fire engine woke up early. The sun was shining in through the fire station door. It's the perfect day to plant a new garden, Red thought as he started his engine.

Rrrrrr. Rrrr-urr-urr. Red's engine sounded funny. Pop! Pop! Pop! Now loud noises were coming out of his exhaust pipe.

As his engine sputtered, Red tried to shrug it off. Hopefully, whatever was wrong would go away, because Red did not want to go to Doc's clinic. He'd never been, but he sure didn't like the idea of being poked and prodded. Some of the tools Doc used were awfully loud. Just the thought of going upset Red's tank.

Red decided to go for a drive. Maybe that would make him feel a bit better.

As he drove
out of town, Red
passed Lightning
McQueen.

"Hey, Red!"
Lightning greeted
him. "How's it
going?"

"Fine," Red
replied shyly. Bang!
Bang!

"Whoa!" exclaimed Lightning. "That can't feel good. You okay?"

"Mmm-hmm," said Red.

Lightning watched as Red drove away. He could hear that Red's
engine wasn't firing right. He's probably afraid to get it checked out,
thought Lightning.

A few minutes later, Lightning got an idea. If he could get Red to race him to the clinic, maybe he could trick him into going inside.

"Hey, Red!" Lightning shouted as he caught up with the fire engine, who was turning around. The little bit that Red had already driven had made him feel worse, so he decided he would go back to town and work on the garden. Maybe that would help.

"You want to race into town?" Lightning asked him. "I'll give you a head start. What do you say?"

"Oh . . ." Hic! "No!" said Red, sputtering. "You're too fast."

"C'mon, Red. I'll even drive backwards, just like Mater taught me," insisted Lightning. "It'll be fun."

"No, thanks," said Red. "Have to plant my flowers."

Pop! Red started driving towards town.

Lightning headed into town, too, to find his friends. They wouldn't want Red to be sick.

Lightning McQueen found everyone at Flo's V8 Café, filling up on breakfast.

"Good morning, mi amigo," Ramone greeted him. "Beautiful day, eh?"

"Yeah, it is," said Lightning, "except for one problem."

"What could that-a be?" asked Luigi, the tyre-shop owner.

"Red's not running right," McQueen explained as he pointed to the fire engine, who was starting to plant a garden across the street. "But he's afraid to go to the clinic."

"Aw, shucks," said Mater the tow truck. "I know how the poor fella feels. I was scared my first time, too! But Doc's a pro. He'll have Red fixed up before he knows what hit him!"

"We've got to get him there first," said Lightning.

"That silly boy," said Flo. "Let me see if I can talk to him."

Flo began to drive towards Red.

Even from a distance,
Flo could hear Red's
engine rumbling.

"Hey there, Red!"
she called out. "You're sounding
a little rough this morning. When was the
last time you went in for a tune-up?"

"Oh, uh . . ."

"That's what I thought," said Flo. "Honey, you need to get yourself
in there."

Red looked down nervously.

"How about," continued Flo, "you go get checked out. Then,
afterwards, come by the café for a free tank of my best fuel?"

"Gee, Flo," said Red. "Thanks, but I'm all right." The truck went
back to his flowers.

"I tell you," Flo said to her friends when she returned to the V8, "that
is one stubborn fire engine."

80

"Don't take it personally, baby," said Ramone, Flo's husband and the owner of Ramone's House of Body Art. "Let me try."

Ramone drove over to Red. "Hey, my friend, you look like you could use some brightening up."

"Hello, Ramone," said Red. "I'm fine."

"No, really, man," Ramone said. "It's today's paint-shop special – a new coat of paint and a custom flame job, free with a visit to Doc's. You'll be the hottest fire engine around."

"Thanks, Ramone . . . but no."

Red continued with his new flower bed. Ramone could see Red wasn't making much progress. So far, he hadn't even planted one flower!

81

Ramone returned to Flo's. "Couldn't talk him into it," he said.

"What that boy needs is some discipline," said Sarge, who had just driven in with his neighbour, Fillmore.

Sarge rolled over behind Red. "Hut two!" roared Sarge.

"Aaaaahh!" screamed Red.

"I order you to go to Doc's in the next five minutes and get yourself a thorough once-over!" Sarge demanded.

Red just looked at Sarge and shook his head.

"Don't you eyeball me!" yelled Sarge. "Get on the street and start rolling, soldier! Move it, move it, move it!"

Red looked down and began to cry.

From across the street at Flo's, everyone could see Sarge's method wasn't working.

"We had better get over there before Red drives away," Lightning said to Sally, who had just rolled up.

The two cars sped over. Mater, Luigi, Guido, Fillmore, Flo and Ramone followed.

"Okay, Sarge!" yelled Lightning. "That's enough."

"Show him a little love, man," said Fillmore.

"Oh, well, I tried," said Sarge. He turned to Red. "I didn't mean to scare you, Red. No hard feelings, I hope."

"It's okay," Red replied, swallowing a sob. After a minute, he stopped crying.

"Oh, it is so-a nice to see two friends make up-a," said Luigi. "I tell you what, Red, since you are my friend, too, I make-a you this-a promise. You go to the clinic, I give you new set of tyres. What you say?"

"Well," said Red thoughtfully, "my tyres are shabby. . . ."

Everyone waited. Was Red finally going to agree to go?

"But I don't think so," the fire truck finished.

Everyone groaned. They had been so close! It looked like they would have to come up with another idea.

Then Mater thought of something. "I'll take you tractor tipping!" the tow truck promised. "Once you knock over a sleeping tractor and hear it snort, you'll be laughing so hard, you'll forget you even went to Doc's."

85

"Thanks, Mater, but no," said Red. "And don't worry, friends, I'll be okay." Red turned away from the other cars and looked back down at his new flowerbed. He sighed. He was so tired and he hadn't got very far.

Bang! Pop, pop, pop! Red's engine gurgled, and more loud noises came out of his exhaust pipe.

"Dad gum!" said Mater. "I reckon that's about the worst sound I ever heard come out of you."

Sally decided it was time for one last try. She inched forward.

"Listen, Red," said Sally. "We all know going to get a tune-up for the first time can be scary. But whatever is wrong could be easy to fix. If you don't go now, it could turn into a bigger problem later. None of us wants you to need a complete overhaul.

We care too much about you."

Red looked back at his friends. He knew what Sally said was true.

"Will you go with me?" he asked Sally.

"Of course I will," she replied.

"We'll all go," said Lightning. "We wouldn't let you go it alone, pal."

Red smiled.

Later that day, Red rolled out of the clinic. All his friends were waiting for him.

"That wasn't so bad," he told them. "I feel great."

Doc followed Red. "He's all fixed up, guys, and healthy as a horse!" Doc proclaimed.

"All right, Red!" said Lightning. "How about that race?"

"Okay," said Red, "and then I'll plant my flowers."

"You go ahead," said Lightning. "I'll be ready when you are."

Red revved his engine. Vroom! It sounded smooth as silk.
He took off.

As Lightning started to catch up, Red turned his siren on full blast.
Woooo-wooooo.

Lightning was so startled that he veered off the road into the bushes.
Sally, Doc and the other cars giggled. Red smiled and
sped forwards. It was good to be running on all cylinders again.

Ka-chOWW!

"I am speed!" Lightning McQueen chanted as he focused
on the dirt track stretched out in front of him. "Is my pit crew ready?"
"Standing by," said Luigi. "Tyres ready!"
"Pit stop!" Guido added happily.

KA-CHOWW!

VAAA-ROOOOM! Lightning revved his engine – and took off!
"Woo-hooo!" he shouted. "It sure is great to zip around this dirt
track after all that fancy stadium stuff. Out here, it's just
me and –"

WHOOSH! "Whoa!" Lightning cried as he spun
out of control. He was headed towards a cactus patch!

"I give you the best tyres, but look – you still wipe out," Luigi remarked as he stared down at Lightning.

"Yeah, thanks," Lightning replied. "Ouch! My turns work perfectly on a real racetrack. Why can't I handle the dirt? I can't wait till my racing stadium is built. I'll be cruising then! Ka-chOWW! Ow-ow-OW!"

"I told ya to steer right to go left. Can't you remember anything, hotshot?" It was Doc. He had been watching the whole time!

"Hey, Doc," replied Lightning. "What brings you out here, besides grumbling about my racing style?"

"That's exactly why I'm here!" Doc shouted back. "Mater, tow your rookie friend out of this mess!"

"Hey, buddy!" called Mater. "I'll have you outta there faster than a runaway tractor slidin' on an oil slick!"

Sure enough, Mater got him up and out of the patch in a jiffy.

"I'm going back to town," Lightning grumbled.

"Now, wait just a second, rookie!" Doc challenged Lightning. "If I'm crew chief, you gotta do things my way. Plus you're on my turf!"

"Whatever," Lightning said. "But first can
I get cleaned up and take some of these prickles
out of my tyres? I think I scratched my paint job –"
   "No!" interrupted Doc. "Try that turn again – unless
it's too much for you, hotshot."

Reluctantly, Lightning stayed.

"New rules," lectured Doc. "No more worrying about your silly paint job. No more whining about a few cactus prickles. And no more rest until you make that turn look easy!"

Lightning tried the turn again . . .
and again . . . and again.
Sometimes he made it, and sometimes he
didn't. "Ow-ow-OW!" he shouted
each time he hit another cactus.

103

"I can do this, I know I can," Lightning said, revving his engine. "Watch me now."

Slowly, he returned to the starting line. Then, more determined than ever, he roared down the dirt track, concentrating on Doc's advice. And when he came to the curve, he glided around the corner – and stayed on the track!

"Ka-chow!" he hooted as he headed towards the finish line.
"Wahoo!" cried Mater. "You did it, buddy!"
"And with style!" added Lightning.

"Congratulations," said Doc.
"You finally listened to some good advice."

"Yeah, the advice of a grumpy old car," Lightning spat back.
Then he turned to Doc and grinned. "Feel like taking a little
spin around the track?"

"Sure, rookie." Doc smiled and sped off. The race was on!

106

AL'S SKY HIGH ADVENTURE

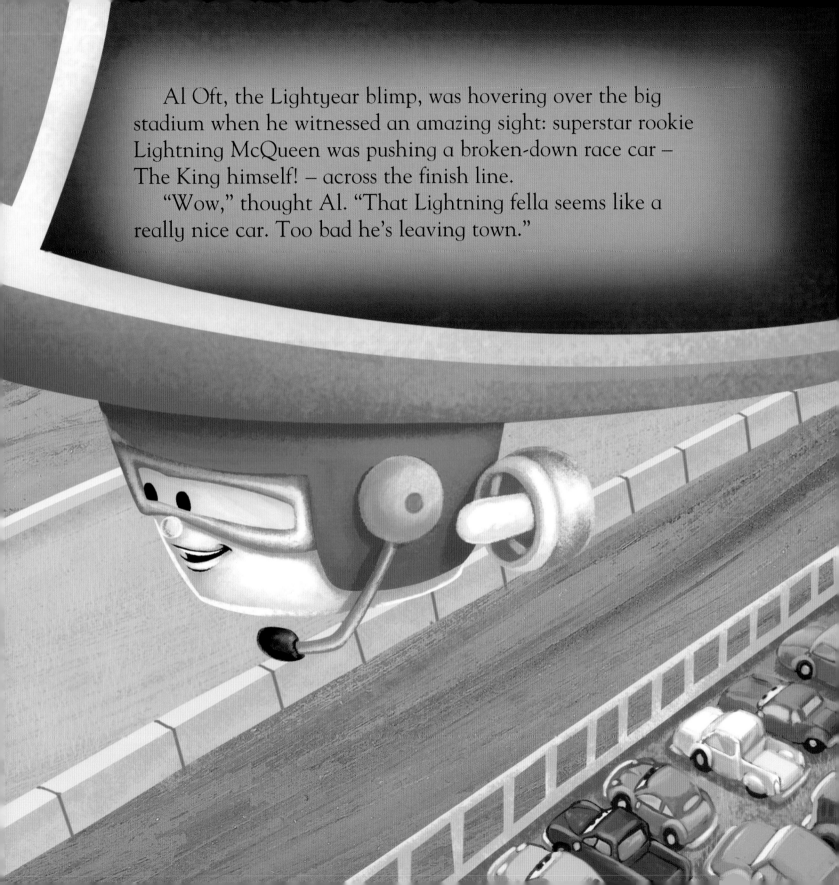

Al Oft, the Lightyear blimp, was hovering over the big stadium when he witnessed an amazing sight: superstar rookie Lightning McQueen was pushing a broken-down race car – The King himself! – across the finish line.

"Wow," thought Al. "That Lightning fella seems like a really nice car. Too bad he's leaving town."

Everyone at the racetrack knew who Al was.
The fans always cheered when he flew overhead.
But he was lonely up in the sky all by himself.

Al couldn't help admiring Lightning's pit crew. It was filled with the rookie's close friends. They had come all the way from Radiator Springs to support Lightning at his big race.

After the race season, Al decided to fly slowly over the countryside, looking at everything below and just enjoying the ride. Sometimes he even helped lost travellers. He had a good view from above and could guide the cars to their destinations.

One day, Al saw a little town below him that looked like the place Lightning had described. He flew low – and spotted Lightning McQueen himself!

"Hey, Lightning!" shouted a rusty old truck. "Lookee there! It's that Lightyear blimp from your big race!"

"Al, it's you! How are you doing, buddy? Welcome to
Radiator Springs!" Lightning called up.

"My name's Mater. Like 'tuh-mater,' without the 'tuh'!"
said the rusty truck. "Wanna help us round up a stray tractor
that busted loose, Mr. Blimp?"

"Yeah," said Lightning. "We can't see where the lost tractor went. But I'll bet you can from up there!"

"Sure," said Al. "What does he look like?"

"A tractor that looks like he's lost," Mater replied.

Sure enough, from high in the sky, Al soon found the lost tractor. He lit up his sign to show Lightning that he had found him.

"Hey, that's great, Al, but we can't get over those big rocks!" Lightning shouted. "Can you see a way for us to get around them?"

Al looked down and all around. Sure enough, he soon found a path the two cars could take to reach the lost tractor. Within minutes, Mater and Lightning were guiding the tractor home.

118

"Now, this calls for a celebration, Al!" Lightning shouted.
"We're having one of our neon cruises tonight. Why don't you join us?"
But Al just looked sadly at Lightning. "I can't cruise,"
he replied. "I'm too big and too high up."
"Sure you can!" said Lightning. "Just turn on your neon and fly low."

That night, Al turned on his sign and flew very low.

As the cars in Radiator Springs looked up at Al, Lightning introduced him. "That's my friend Al Oft, the Lightyear blimp. Just look at him. He's got the best neon you've ever seen."

"And you sure know how to cruise – low and slow!" Ramone told Al.

Al smiled. He was having the most fun he'd ever had. And with all his new friends, he knew he'd never be lonely again.

BLUE RAMONE

"Dum-da-dee-dum," Ramone hummed in his body shop.
  "Hey there, buddy! Are you painting yourself again?"
It was Lightning, and Mater was with him.
  "Yeah, blue is Flo's favourite colour. It's for her birthday party,"
Ramone replied. "And I plan on staying this colour for an entire week!"

"Gee whiz!" shouted Mater. "I've never seen you stay one colour for a whole week!"

"That's not a bad idea, there, Ramone," Lightning said. "You know, when I open my new headquarters in Radiator Springs, you'll have to paint someone besides yourself all day long."

"No problem," Ramone said, but Lightning wondered. How long could Ramone stay one colour?

That night, the whole town gathered for a cruise down Main Street in honour of Flo's birthday. But where was Ramone?

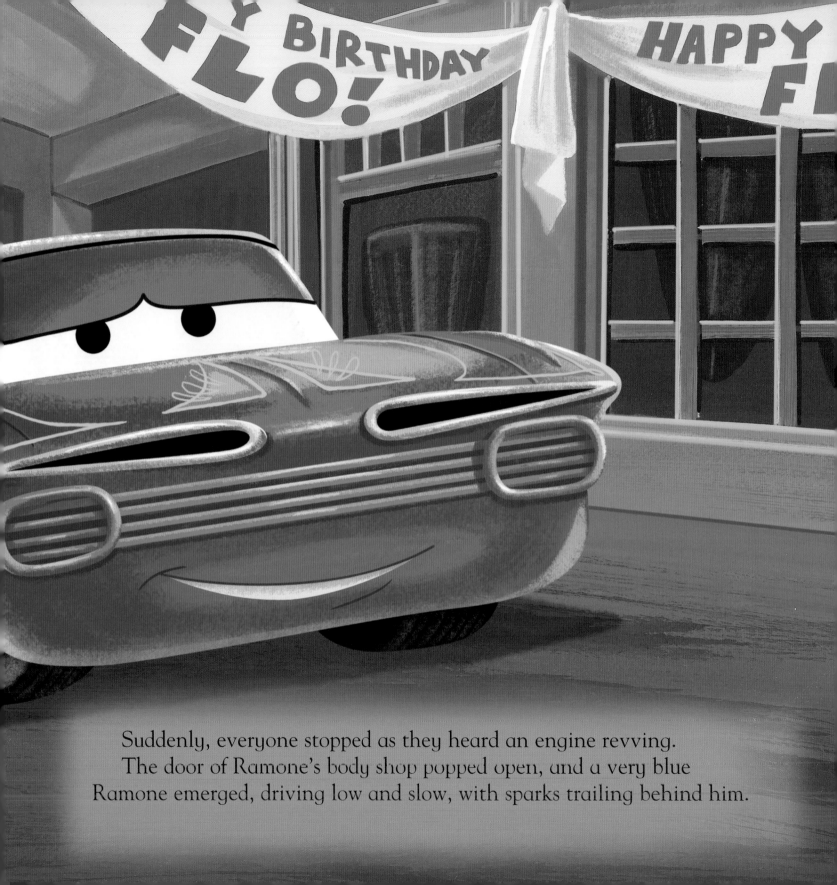

Suddenly, everyone stopped as they heard an engine revving.
The door of Ramone's body shop popped open, and a very blue
Ramone emerged, driving low and slow, with sparks trailing behind him.

"Oh, Ramone!" Flo exclaimed. "You painted yourself blue!"
"You like it?" Ramone asked his wife.
"I sure do," Flo said, smiling. "It's still my favourite.
Now, are you going to take
me on a birthday cruise
or what?"

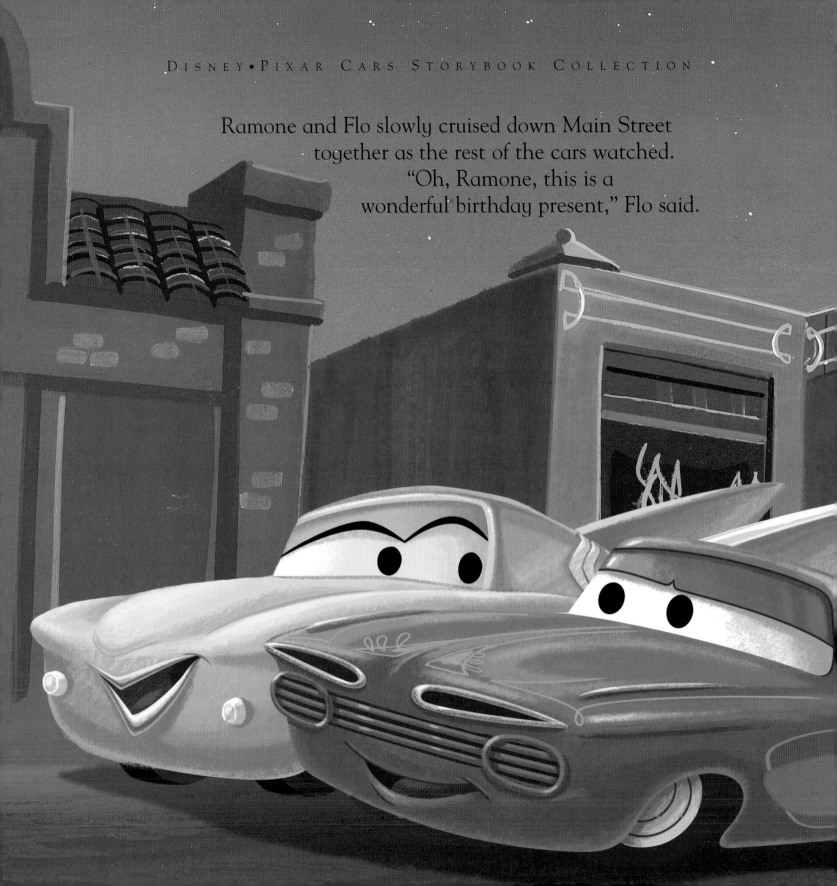

Ramone and Flo slowly cruised down Main Street
together as the rest of the cars watched.
"Oh, Ramone, this is a
wonderful birthday present," Flo said.

Then Mater spoke up. "Hey, Ramone, do you think you can keep that promise you made to Lightning today?"

Ramone stopped short. "Hey, everybody! I've got an announcement to make!" he shouted. "In honour of Flo's birthday, I promise to stay blue for one full week!"

Everyone gasped. "Are you sure?" asked Flo.

"I'm surer than sure," Ramone replied.

The next day, Ramone got up early and started cleaning his shop to
get ready for the customers who would soon be coming to town.
But after a couple of hours, he was finished.
He was tempted to paint himself a new colour. Then he remembered his
promise. So he went over to Flo's instead.

"Hey, baby, you want a quart of oil?" Flo asked Ramone.

"Yeah, thanks," Ramone said. Then he added, "Do you want me to give you a new paint job?"

"Oh, honey, thanks, but no," said Flo. "I have all this work to do."

"Looking sharp, soldier!" Sarge called out to Ramone.

"Thanks, Sarge," said Ramone. "Do you want a paint job? I haven't seen you in a different colour in ages!"

"No, sir!" Sarge declared. "No time. I have to get my boot camp ready for when the customers come to town."

135

Ramone stayed blue the next day and the next. He kept
asking all the cars in town if they wanted paint jobs, but they
were all too busy. Ramone couldn't stand it any longer. He had
to paint something!

"Ramone! What's wrong with you, baby?" Flo said one day.
But Ramone just shrugged and looked at his paint supplies.

"Ramone, listen to me. If you want to paint yourself a new colour, just go right ahead and do it."

"But I made a promise," Ramone said sadly.

"No, a happy, freshly-painted Ramone made that promise," Flo said with a sigh. "I miss that Ramone. Just be yourself."

"Yeah," said Mater. "Just be yourself. We like ya that way." Ramone turned around. It seemed as if the whole town was there to encourage him.

Ramone wasted no time. He happily went to work painting himself every colour he could find.

"Good to see the old Ramone back!" shouted Lightning.

"You can say that again," Mater said, smiling. "In fact, I will. You can say that again!"

SARGE'S BOOT CAMP

"AttenTION!" Sarge yelled. Guido and Luigi stopped short and stared at Sarge, waiting for orders.

"First gear!" Sarge shouted. Guido and Luigi started moving slowly. "Second gear! Third gear! Fourth gear!"

Luigi raced down Main Street with Guido speeding behind.

"Hey!" yelled Sheriff, turning on his lights and siren. "Slow down, fellas!"

Just then, Lightning McQueen pulled up.

"Sorry, Sheriff," Lightning said. "This may be my fault. You see, I told Sarge that I was setting up my headquarters here in town –"

"And I'm starting a training camp for all the 4x4s that are headed this way!" Sarge interrupted.

"And you're practising with Guido and Luigi?"
Sheriff looked doubtfully at the two little cars.

"They're ready and eager," Sarge replied.

"Fine." Sheriff sighed and turned off his siren and lights. "Just take them off the main road if you're going to be speeding."

Just then a big, brand-new 4x4 rolled into town.

"Hi," said the 4x4. "I'm T.J."

"Look at those tyres," whispered Luigi. "He needs whitewalls."

"Pit stop?" Guido asked eagerly.

"Welcome to Radiator Springs, T.J.!" Sarge
yelled out to the newcomer. "You've reached the home of my
boot camp!"

"Hey, there! Thanks for the welcome," T.J. replied. "But I'm not here for any training. No, sir."

Sarge rolled right up to the 4x4 and faced him head-on. "Perhaps you misunderstood me. That was an ORDER, soldier!"

"Yes, sir!" T.J. replied.

"Car camp!" Luigi shouted happily. "It will be tough! But don't worry. Guido and I are fully prepared to change your tyres at any time."

T.J. gasped. "You mean I might get a flat?"

"You will if you don't change that attitude!" exclaimed Sarge. "Now, let's get going!"

Sarge led the group out of town to a rocky dirt road.

"Oh, no!" T.J. complained. "I've already got dirt in my grille!"

"No talking! Just follow me!" shouted Sarge. "Now . . . first gear! Second gear! Third gear!"

"Ooooo! Ah-ah-ah-ah!" cried the 4x4. "This is so bumpy that my spark plugs are shaking loose. And my treads! Can anybody see my treads? They must be wearing out!"

"Pit stop?" Guido asked eagerly.

"Come on, T.J.," said Luigi. "If Guido can do it, so can you!"

149

Next Sarge led the group to a river. "A tough 4x4 should be able to cross a riverbed!" Sarge shouted. "Now, go, go, go!"

"Eeee!" said T.J., dipping his tyre into the water. "It's cold!"

"Just follow Guido," whispered Luigi.

After a lot more complaining, T.J. followed and barely made it across the river.

"Okay, team!" said Sarge. "It's time for the final drill. We're going down that slope and across that big, muddy puddle. Then we'll call it a day."

T.J. gasped. He could lose control going too fast down the hill! Plus he would get mud all over his rims!

Down, down, down they went. Guido and Luigi zigzagged slowly, while T.J. lost control and careered down the hill.

"I'm gonna flip over!" he cried. "I'm gonna flip over!"

"Hit the brakes!" Sarge called out to T.J. "Show a bit of courage, soldier!"

Soon Sarge, Guido and Luigi were at the bottom of the hill, crossing the mud puddle. T.J. hesitated.

"Come on!" Luigi called to T.J. "You're a 4x4! This should be no problem."

T.J. thought about it and then he laughed out loud. "I'm dirty, my paint is scratched, and I'm tired. But I can do it! Thanks, Guido. Thanks, Luigi."

"Now hit the showers!" Sarge shouted. "We've got a big day tomorrow!"

"Sir! Yes, sir!" T.J. yelled.

Luigi and Guido looked up the hill in front of them. It seemed awfully steep.

"Come on, guys! Hop onto my roof rack! I'll give you a ride," offered T.J. Together the cars raced right up the hill and all the way back to town – ready for another day of Sarge's boot camp!

ALSO AVAILABLE IN THE SERIES...

Storybook Collection

Storybook Collection

Storybook Collection

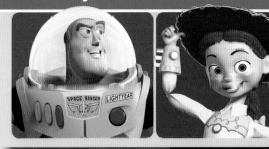

Storybook Collection

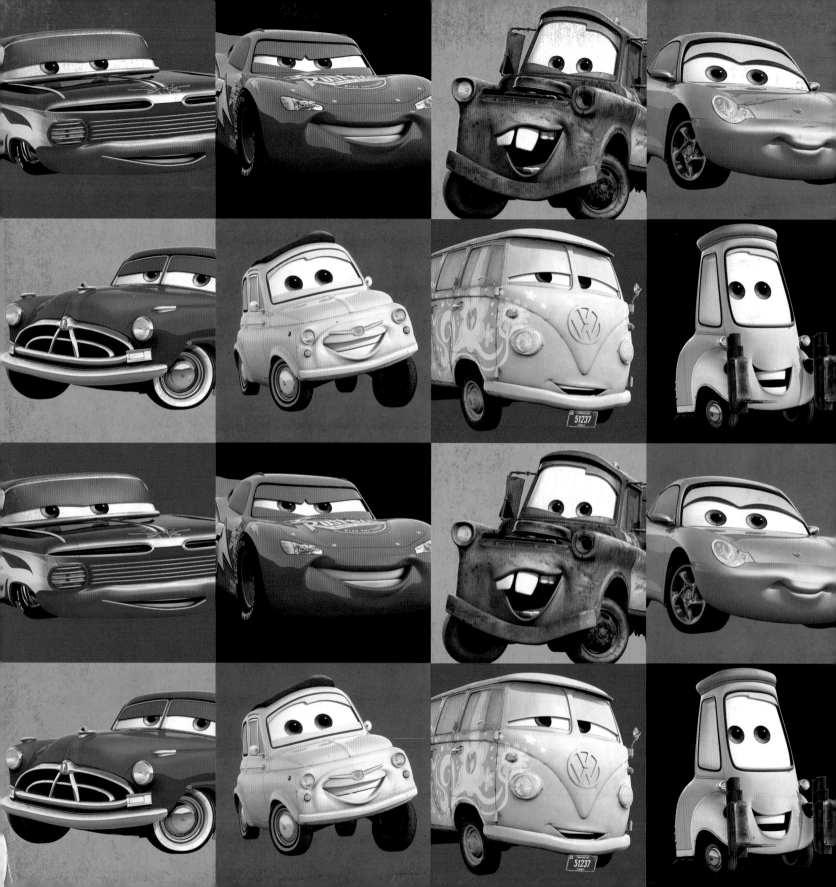